This book
belongs to:

....

....

Baby Bear's Adventures

BRIMAX

Originally published in Australia by Thomas C. Lothian Pty Ltd and in Great Britain by Brimax as:

Baby Bear Goes to the Zoo (2000) © Lorette Broekstra

Baby Bear Goes to the Beach (2001) © Lorette Broekstra

Baby Bear Goes Camping (2001) © Lorette Broekstra

Baby Bear Goes to the Farm (2002) © Lorette Broekstra

This edition first published in Great Britain in 2002 by Brimax,
an imprint of Octopus Publishing Group Ltd
2-4 Heron Quays, London E14 4JP
© Octopus Publishing Group Ltd 2002

A CIP catalogue record for this book is available
from the British Library.

ISBN 1 85854 584 6

Printed in China

Contents

NOTE TO PARENTS

Baby Bear has lots of adventures and meets a variety of interesting creatures and characters in these bright, fun, and simple stories. Your child will be enchanted by the amusing stories and beautiful illustrations and will want to read them over and over again.

The stories can also be used to help your child learn more about the world, build vocabulary, and develop core skills. Read the stories together and ask your child questions about them to maximize enjoyment and learning potential. For instance, in *Baby Bear goes to the Zoo*, Baby Bear learns that he should never go off by himself and you can use this to teach your child, too. While on a camping trip, Baby Bear realizes that there is no need to be scared of the dark. In his adventures on the farm, Baby Bear counts from one to ten and you can use the story to help your child learn numbers.

We hope you and your child enjoy *Baby Bear's Adventures*.

Baby Bear
goes to the ZOO

et's go to the zoo,' said Mama Bear to Baby Bear.

They quickly packed a picnic lunch
and set off for the zoo.

They decided to visit the giraffe first.
'Look at his lovely long neck,' said Mama Bear.

'What's that?' asked Baby Bear,
brushing his ear with his paw.
'It's a butterfly!' said Mama Bear.

Just then the butterfly fluttered away.
Baby Bear scampered after it.

He chased the butterfly past the elephants,

past the lions,

past the zebras,

and past the monkeys,
until the butterfly disappeared over a wall.

Poor Baby Bear was all alone!
He began to cry, but then he heard,
'Baby Bear! Baby Bear!'

Baby Bear ran to see who was calling him.

'You're not my mama!' said Baby Bear,
'Why are you calling me?'
'I'm Mama Panda Bear and I'm calling
my baby for lunch.'

'Oh!' said Baby Bear sadly,
and he set off to find his mama.
He hadn't gone very far before he heard,

'Baby Bear! Baby Bear!'

Baby Bear ran to see who was calling him.

'You're not my mama!' said Baby Bear,
'Why are you calling me?'
'I'm Mama Brown Bear and I'm calling
my baby for lunch.'

'Oh!' said Baby Bear disappointedly,
and he set off to find his mama.
He hadn't gone very far before he heard,

'Baby Bear! Baby Bear!'

Baby Bear ran to see who was calling him.

'You're not my mama!' said Baby Bear,
'Why are you calling me?'
'I'm Mama Polar Bear and I'm calling
my baby for lunch.'

'Oh!' said Baby Bear helplessly,
and he set off to find his mama.
He hadn't gone very far before he heard,

'Baby Bear! Baby Bear!'
'There you are Baby Bear! I've found you!'

It was Mama!

Baby Bear ran all the way

to meet his mama.

'Where have you been?' asked Mama Bear.
'It's lunchtime!'
'I know,' said Baby Bear.

Baby Bear
goes to the
Beach

t was a lovely day and Baby Bear was going
to the beach with his mama and papa.
He had already packed his beach bag and
was waiting for Papa Bear to find his hat.

'This is a good spot,' said Baby Bear
when they got to the beach.

He sat down and unpacked his ball,
his bucket, his shovel and his sunscreen.

The water looked great, but Baby Bear
decided to build a sandcastle first.

He filled buckets with sand
and piled them higher and higher until
he had built a beautiful sandcastle.

'That looks great!' said Papa Bear.

'It's wonderful. All it needs is a special shell right there,'
said Mama Bear pointing to the top of the castle.
'You're right!' said Baby Bear and he set off to find one.

Baby Bear searched . . .

and searched.

'Phew! It's getting hot,' he said to himself.
'Time for a swim.'

Baby Bear ran and jumped into the sea.

He splashed about in the cool clear water,

on his back . . .

on his belly . . .

and THEN he dived right under.

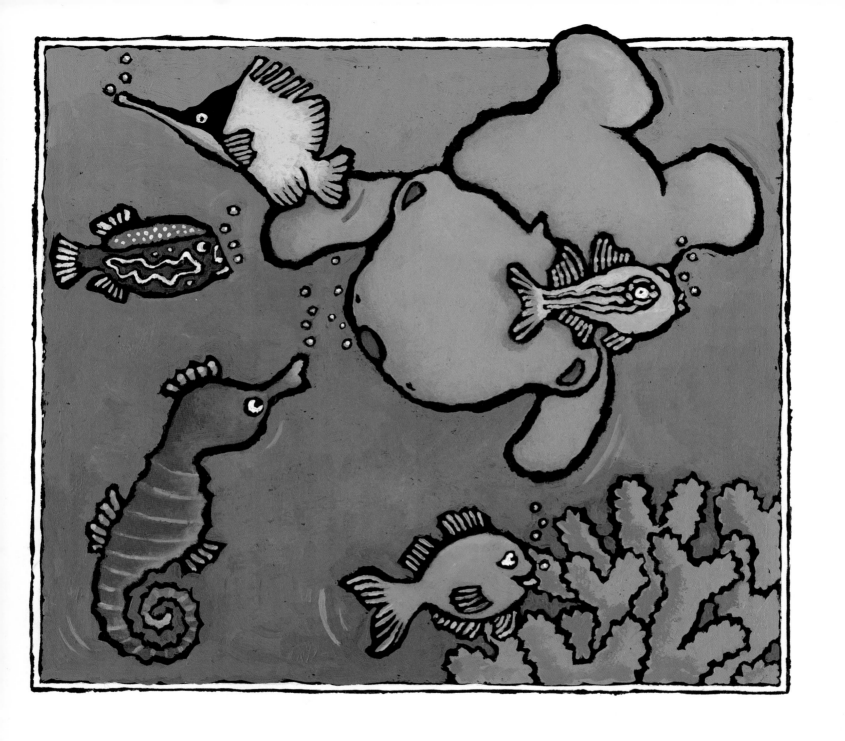

'Hello,' he said to a seahorse swimming by.
'Hello,' said the seahorse. 'Nice to meet you.'

'Ouch!' said Baby Bear when he felt
something nip him on the toe.
'Sorry,' said a crab, and he went on his way.

'You're in a hurry,' said Baby Bear to an octopus.
'Yes,' said the octopus, 'I can hardly keep up with myself.'

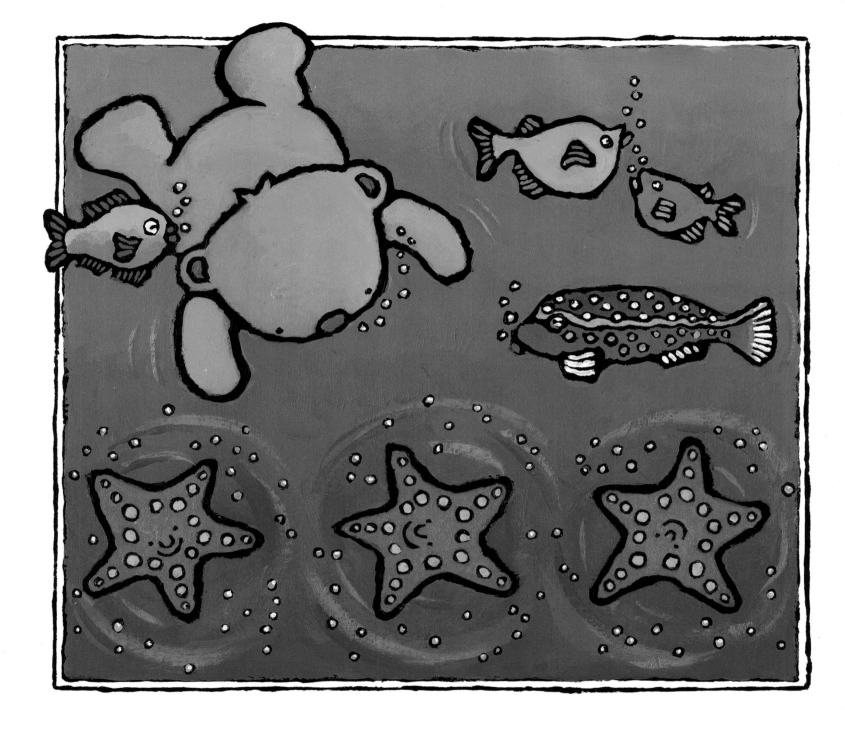

'That looks like fun,' said Baby Bear to a
spotted starfish doing cartwheels as he passed by.
'I'd like to try that.'

And he did a cartwheel, too.

He stopped when he heard a snap-snapping sound.
'Don't worry,' said a lobster. 'It's only me.'

Baby Bear clapped his hands when he saw
two jellyfish doing a lovely dance together.

'It's so beautiful down here,'
thought Baby Bear watching a school of fish
come swimming his way.

When they were gone Baby Bear looked down
and saw the most beautiful shell lying on the sea bed.
He'd found just what his sandcastle needed.

He picked up the shell

and quickly swam back

to find his mama and papa.

'Hi, Mama. Hi, Papa,' said Baby Bear.
'Hi,' said Mama Bear.
'What have you been doing?' asked Papa Bear.

'Oh, nothing much,' said Baby Bear,
'but I found a really nice shell for my sandcastle.'

Baby Bear
goes
Camping

t was an exciting day for Baby Bear.
He was going on his first camping trip.

He couldn't wait to start putting up
his very own tent.

After the tents were up and the beds were made
Papa Bear said, 'Let's go for a walk.'

On their walk Baby Bear said, 'Hello,' to an owl,

'Good afternoon,' to a frog,

'Hi,' to a bat

and, 'How do you do?' to a porcupine.

When they returned from their walk they were feeling
very hungry, so Papa Bear started a fire.

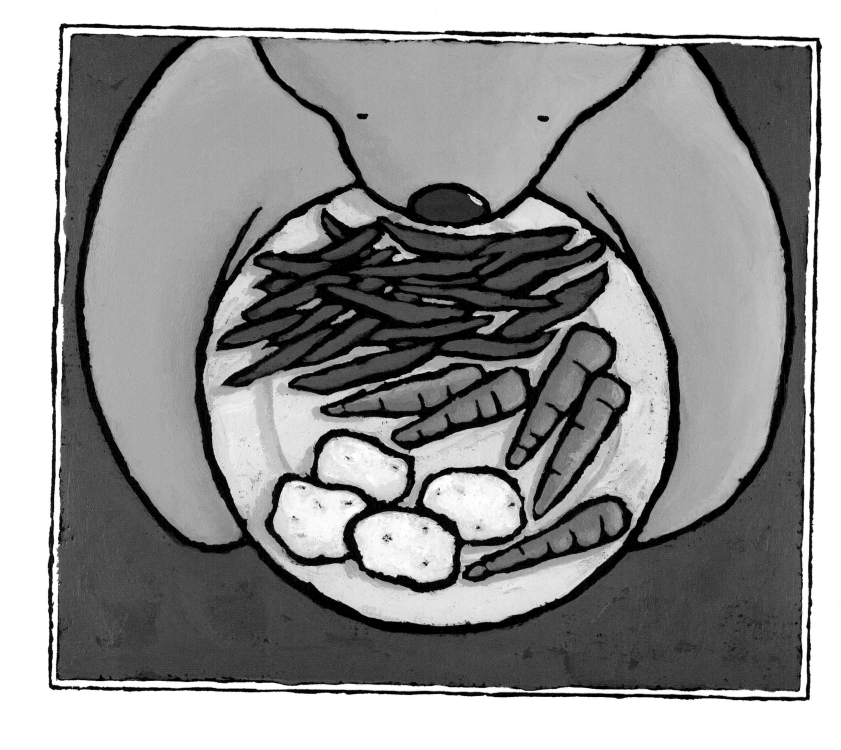

He cooked potatoes, carrots and green beans.
It was a delicious meal.

'Ah,' sighed Baby Bear, 'camping is good fun.'

'And very tiring.' He yawned.

It was bedtime for Baby Bear.
'Goodnight, Papa Bear.
Goodnight, Mama Bear,' said Baby Bear.

'Goodnight,' said Papa Bear.
'Sleep tight,' said Mama Bear.

But when Baby Bear got into bed he couldn't sleep.
There were too many strange noises.
'Whoo, whoo.' Baby Bear shivered.

'Ribbit! Ribbit!' Baby Bear shook.

And then he saw a huge shadow on
the side of his tent,

and another one on the other side!

Poor Baby Bear was feeling very scared.
He stumbled,

and started to fall.
'Ow!' said Baby Bear as he fell right out of the tent.

He looked up and saw Bat.
'Oh, it was you making that scary shadow!' he said.

Then he saw Porcupine.
'And it was you making that other shadow on my tent.'

'Whoo!' said Owl.
'Oh!' said Baby Bear. 'It was you making that sound.'

'Ribbit!'
'And that was you, Frog!'

'We just came to say goodnight to you, Baby Bear,'
said Bat, Porcupine, Owl and Frog.

Baby Bear laughed. 'Goodnight,' he said.

He went back into his tent,
climbed into his sleeping bag and had
his best sleep ever.

Baby Bear
goes to the Farm

One day a letter arrived for Baby Bear. It was from Farmer Bear. His dog Rosie was missing and he needed help on the farm.

'Please, may I go?' asked Baby Bear.
'Of course,' said Papa Bear. 'I'll take you there.'

Papa Bear drove Baby Bear to the farm.
'I'll pick you up at the end of the day,' said Papa Bear.

Baby Bear found Farmer Bear near the haystack.
'I'm glad you could come,' said Farmer Bear.

'What would you like me to do?' asked Baby Bear.
Farmer Bear gave Baby Bear a list.

'**1**. Milk the cow,' read Baby Bear.
He milked the cow and filled **one** bucket

with creamy white milk.

'**2**. Brush the donkeys,' read Baby Bear.
He brushed the **two** donkeys.

'Heehaw,' they said, 'that felt good.'

'**3**. Feed the geese,' read Baby Bear.
He fed the **three** geese.

'Honk! Honk! Thank you,' they said.

'**4**. Bring the horses to the field,' read Baby Bear.
He let the **four** horses out of the stable

and brought them to the field.

'**5**. Round up the sheep,' read Baby Bear.
He rounded up the **five** sheep

and put them in their pen.

'**6**. Collect the eggs,' read Baby Bear.
He collected **six** eggs.

'Cluck. Cluck. Hello, Baby Bear,' said the chickens.

'**7**. Gather the corn,' read Baby Bear.
He picked **seven** ears of corn.

They looked delicious.

'**8**. Check the piglets,' read Baby Bear.
He counted — one, two, three, four, five, six,
seven, **eight** piglets.

They all seemed fine.

'**9**. Pick some apples,' read Baby Bear.
He picked **nine** ripe, red apples.

Baby Bear had finished all the jobs on his list.
He went to tell Farmer Bear.

But on the way, he heard a yapping sound.

It was coming from behind the haystack.
Rosie! He'd found Rosie.

He'd found Rosie and **ten** baby puppies!